W9-CFD-627

Inside Citizens Bank Park, the Phillie Phanatic was reading a big history book. "Mom, I have a history test about Philadelphia tomorrow and I'm really nervous that I won't get any of the answers right."

"Oh Phanatic, you'll do fine. You LOVE Philadelphia," Phoebe Phanatic said. "I know, but learning history can be hard because everything happened so long ago when things were so much different," the Phanatic replied.

Phoebe had an idea.  She left the room and came back with something the
Phanatic had never seen before.  Phoebe said, "Try this, Phanatic.
It's a virtual reality time travel helmet.  My mother gave
it to me when I was a girl. Now I want you to have it."

The Phanatic looked confused. Phoebe continued, "When I was your age, I had a hard time learning history, too. This time travel helmet helps because it makes you feel like you can travel back in time."

The Phanatic strapped the helmet on top of his head.
Phoebe handed him a remote control. "Just set
this dial to the period of time you would
like to travel to," she said.

"In school, we're learning all about the early days of Philadelphia," said the Phanatic. He set the dial to "COLONIAL PHILADELPHIA" and looked through the viewfinder.

Suddenly, the Phanatic felt like he was standing on a
cobblestone road in the middle of colonial Philadelphia.
People all around were surprised to see
the furry green mascot.

The Phanatic looked down at his clothes. He was wearing clothes like the people wore in his history book. "This is better than any video game I've ever played!" the Phanatic exclaimed.

The Phanatic saw a group of men hard at work laying bricks.
"What are you building?" he asked. One of the men replied,
"We're building the country's first library and we need all the
help we can get." The Phanatic was happy to lend a hand.

After the library was built, the Phanatic helped build the country's first public school, the first hospital and the first firehouse. "Just like the Phillies," the Phanatic thought, "Philadelphia is first in a lot of things."

The Phillie Phanatic saw a familiar face from his history book. It was Ben Franklin, and he was flying a kite. In the distance, the Phanatic heard the sound of rumbling thunder. "Hi Ben! It sounds like a storm is coming. Why are you flying a kite?"

"I'm testing my theory that there is electricity in lightning,"
Ben said.  As raindrops started to fall, he handed the
Phanatic the kite.  "Hold this, Phanatic, while
I go inside to get an umbrella."

After Ben left, lightning hit the kite and gave
the Phanatic the shock of his life.

Ben came running out of his house. "Phanatic, you discovered electricity!" he yelled. "No, Ben, I think electricity discovered me," replied the woozy mascot.

"My, my, Phanatic, look at your clothes. They are a mess," Ben said.
"You look like you could use a new shirt. There's a seamstress
in town. Her name is Betsy Ross and I'm sure
she will be able to help you."

When they arrived at Betsy Ross' house, Ben introduced the Phillie Phanatic to Betsy. "What are you sewing, Betsy?" "I was asked to make the country's new flag but I don't know what colors to use or what the new flag should look like," Betsy said.

Ben said, "The Phanatic needs a new shirt. Can you make him one?" "What do you want your shirt to look like?" she asked the Phanatic. "The shirt I normally wear has stars and stripes on it," the Phanatic said. Soon, Betsy was hard at work cutting the pattern and sewing it all together with her needle and thread.

"Wow, this is perfect!" the Phanatic said. Suddenly, Betsy's
eyes lit up. "Stars and stripes! Now I've got an idea for
what the country's new flag should look like!
Thanks, Phanatic!"

A little while later, Betsy was finished sewing. "How does it look?" she asked, holding up a beautiful red, white and blue flag. "I love it!" the Phanatic said.

Ben and the Phillie Phanatic walked to Independence Hall. Ben said, "Today, we are going to sign the Declaration of Independence right here in Philadelphia. Would you like to come inside and be a part of history, Phanatic?" "You bet I would!" the excited mascot said.

When the Phanatic walked inside, it was like his history book had come to life. There was Thomas Jefferson, John Adams and the rest of the Founding Fathers. They were all getting ready to sign the Declaration of Independence.

"Hey, Phanatic," Thomas Jefferson called out.
"Do you want to sign it, too?"

The Phanatic signed his name and a new country -
the United States of America - was born!

"Great job, Phanatic," Thomas said. "Now it's your job to go tell the people that we have started a new country." "How am I going to do that?" the Phanatic asked. "You must ring the Liberty Bell, of course!" Thomas answered.

The Phanatic remembered that he had his special time travel helmet on and it was getting late. "Ben, I've got to go but I want to thank you for helping me with my history lesson," the Phanatic said. "It was my pleasure," Ben said. "History can be fun when you feel like a part of it."

When the Phanatic took off his helmet, he found himself back in his room with his mom, Phoebe. "That time travel helmet really works," the Phanatic said. "I built the country's first library, I discovered electricity and I signed the Declaration of Independence."

The next day, the Phanatic came running into the house looking for Phoebe. "Mom, Mom, I got an A+ on my history test!" the Phanatic exclaimed. "Good for you, Phanatic," Phoebe said.

"Mom, can you get the time travel helmet for me and some glue?"
the Phanatic asked Phoebe. "Why do you want me to
get that, Phanatic?" Phoebe asked.

"I've got to go back to colonial Philadelphia
and fix that bell!" the Phanatic said.